eccentricities:
a collection of poetry and stories

by Lee Weldon Bailiff

Published in the United States of America by Lee Weldon Bailiff

ISBN (print): 978-0-9857917-3-5
ISBN (e-book): 978-0-9857917-4-2

dedicated to my family

eccentricities:
a collection of poetry and stories

Story Contents

1.

Within a day unlike another
I met a lady who was unique
And when we entertained each other
We could not help but take a peek

Within the eye of the other's mind
To see the dreams that dwelt therein
Treasures and love we hoped to find
And conversations describing when

Our hearts quit trying to resist
Permitting the other's words to touch
The longing for a state of bliss
Recognizing there could ne'er be too much

Contact between these lovers new
Too many moments to some, to us: too few

2.

this day's events, when i sit and reflect,
convince my heart you're the queen of desire;
for no woman compares to your form, so perfect
my eyes are ensnared as two moths to a fire.

my spirit in comfort, your voice envelops;
my dreams with joy, your smile inflates.
from my truest love, a passion develops
warmth greater than a star creates.

discovering with you life's sweeter taste,
a satisfaction we both may savor,
where not a moment goes to waste,
experiencing together our love's flavor...

your attention my peace finds necessary,
your affection my purest accessory.

3.

remembering every moment of joy created
by the interaction of your soul with mine
results in a restless heart sated
by the taste of love's intoxicating wine

drunk on the internal sensation
born from your laughing spirit
an involuntary gesticulation
as my body tenses a bit

in reaction to my daydream nerves
sending pleasure to my mind's muscles
dancing across your subtle curves
to the rhythm of your body's rustles

i dance with you to the music of desire
i dance with you, my love, inspired

4.

the belly of absence's beast became upset with me.
i refused to digest preconceived notions,
and so reality became quite the monstrosity
as it attempted to complicate my devotions.

always and ever constantly shone the light upon your
face;
your smile lit the lantern of my dedication,
and every effort of reality to obscure or erase
you from my life became its hopeless situation.

tell me you love me, reveal your truth to my mind
show me you love me, reveal your body to my eyes
sway your hips and tease my senses until they find
that your love is clothed by purity's disguise.

my eyes will touch what absence forbids.
my imagination will accomplish what distance has
hid.

5.

there's a flower in Houston, Texas, alluring to my
senses
she blooms throughout each season, and i lower my
defenses
when her heavenly aroma ensnares my bewitched
mind
i guarantee that only she can make me leave my cares
behind

her petals are the softest pink, her stems are smooth
and nice
her nectar is a pleasant drink i know is worth the
steepest price
her bloom, devoid of blemish. her name upon my
lips.
her thorns all vanish when i draw near - so pleasant
to my fingertips

the satisfaction i obtain from her, no instrument can
measure

for who can possibly quantify the extent of my heart's
pleasure
my hands both seek to fill themselves with nothing
but her form
as my daydreams pull a sunrise from within absence's
storm

my love is true and constant, desire enflames my
mind
her passion cures my dreams when my mind's eye
becomes blind

6.

my eyes inhale your beauty's breath
and nourish the lungs of my contentment with the
oxygen of your form

there's a shadow of a dream of a thought of a memory
i may have had when i was young
(like a cold breeze down the back of my neck when
i'm wearing a winter coat)
reminding me of a feeling my heart may have had
when i was too immature to know
that sometimes fear and hope and love and joy and
doubt and strength and vulnerability
all share the same definition

my ears drink deep your beauty's voice
and feel the liquid of your gentle sound flow down
deep towards my soul's stomach

there's a glimmer of a pang of a muscle remembering
a burning within my chest
(like standing under a hot shower with icy cold feet)

i recall the throb of a pain i think i had at one time or
another
and i wonder where it went when you sent it away
from me
with three words born from eight letters

7.

The finger of her voice
rests upon the pulse of my soul
and her sunrise smile
rains drops of light
upon my daydream summer.
Warmth radiates from her
into my open heart.

I drink deep by choice
her song, possessing my whole
form and being, while
my face feels the bite
of the cold breath of winter.
Yet, I remain warm within the center
of her generous heart.

I don't worry about
ever losing her to doubt
or seeing her lose hope and surrender.
For there isn't another
I've ever discovered

who wears faith like the snow wears December.

8.

I want to dive into the deep of you and glow within
the dark of you
Discover the true of you and be the morning to the
dew of you
Through it all, fly or fall
Through it all, speed or stall
Through it all, I always call for you

For you

I want to dream the night, breathe the light, see the
bright and flee the trite
I want to dream the smile, breathe the style, see the
guile, and flee denial

I need to feast upon the joy you bring and dance to
the song you sing
Discover the perfect thing that wears your
contentment like a ring
Through it all, fly or fall
Through it all, speed or stall

Through it all, I always call for you

I want to dream the night, breathe the light, see the
bright and flee the trite
I want to dream the smile, breathe the style, see the
guile and flee denial

For you

Through it all, fly or fall
Through it all, speed or stall
Through it all, I always call for you
Through it all, I'll always call for you

For you
For you

9.

when you're on my mind
i can't think straight

you infect my heart
with the germ of hope

when you're in my life
i can't walk straight

you inebriate my heart
with a bottle of joy

and i sing like a desperate man who's forgotten the
sound of his own voice

i strain my ears to hear the echoes

and i tremble when the reverberations carry your alto
notes holding hands with my tenor

a man content may hunger still

a man at peace may flee a state of rest

you're my adventure

and you thrill me

10.

i stand underneath a steel wool sky
watching as the snow blinds my mind's eye;
its touch - all my dreams feel before they die.

and the beat of my heart tries in vain
to knock on the door of your perception
knowing it's trapped within a sweet self-deception
knowing you're not near enough
for your ear to hear enough
of what i'm sayin'

i walk underneath a steel wool sky
feeling gravel underfoot as i walk by;
its sound - all my dreams hear before they die.

and the pupils of my eyes try in vain
to pierce the veil of hesitation
board a jet, fly to the source of my elation
knowing this isn't enough
for me to feel enough
of what you're sayin'

my mind sweats with fear
for the day that draws near
when you disappear

my heart taps its finger
at the nerves that linger
around this silent harbinger

this specter of doubt...
will i eventually have to go without
the one i care so much about...

?

so i anchor my hope on the stone
surrounding the shore of my memory
knowing that as long as it's with me
you'll never really leave and i'll never really be
alone...

11.

sometimes life gets in the way
of all the words i want to say
and everything i've done today
doesn't matter as much as i thought it did

all the patterns that i think i see
sometimes confuse the heart of me
into thinking things that cannot be
are true and right and triumphantly solid

my daydream tongue tastes a memory
of something that never happened to me
as though it was as real as reality
my mind swallowing a morsel of image

and my distracted ears hear a siren song
sung by a mouth whose woman belongs
to a shape that reminds me to come along
and take shelter from potential soul-damage

i desperately seek to remove empty space
from between my desire and the end of the race

that my yearning is running at too quick a pace
for my eyes to take blurs into focus

and i try not to stumble when obstacles come
rolling and strolling from where they come from
to trip up the feet that are seeking the drum
beating slowly, steadily calming the fuss

felt within and without the entirety
of the me that resides in the me of me
where i never let anyone hear or see
any details or feel anything certain

but an angel that lives where my mind is at peace
casts a line at this single, most secretive beast
and takes the unknown from whom knew it least
to bring light from behind honesty's curtain

so beauty told truth to be bold and shun fear
to grab hold of a dream and attract more dreams near
to the place where the beauty said she held them most
dear

within the embrace
of

a
smile

The Story of Five Mornings

There lived a young man, alone on the edge of a crystal sea.

One morning, the young man stood at the point where the stretching water finally started creeping back along the white sand towards the distant waves. The water touched his toes.

He stared at the horizon and the horizon asked him: "For what are you searching?"

"A dream," his soul replied, without his mind having time for a single thought.

The days came and the nights went.

One morning, the grown man stood at the point where he could best regard the gray tumult on the horizon. The sun shone, but the horizon wore clouds and danced within storm. The breeze kissed his face.

He stared at the gray water and the storms asked him: "For what are you searching?"

"A life," his soul replied, without his mind having time for a single thought.

The days came and the nights went.

One morning, the husband stood at the point where his wife could find him. She approached from his right and gently took his hand. He held it and thought about how soft it was. He looked in her eyes and saw constellations. She kissed his hand.

He stared at the horizon and the horizon asked him: "For what are you searching?"

"A calling," his soul replied, without his mind having time for a single thought.

The days came and the nights went.

One morning, the father stood at the point where his children were playing. His wife sat on the white sand, playing with their infant. The older children ran. Their laughter carried joy in buckets. His children hugged his legs.

He stared at the crystal sea and the water asked him: "For what are you searching?"

"Comprehension," his soul replied, without his mind having time for a single thought.

The days came and the nights went.

One morning, the old man stood at the point where his wife laid was laid to rest. He could still feel her hand in his, even after the years alone. His pockets held letters of endearment from his children and grandchildren. They held the first words of love he and his wife had written to each other. They held pictures. A trail of tears painted each cheek.

He stared at the gray clouds on the horizon and the storms asked him: "For what are you searching?"

"Nothing," he heard his voice replying, without his mind having time for a single thought. "I am only remembering."

"What do you remember?" the storms asked.

He thought. He remembered. He spoke:

"Love."

12.

he sat across from a woman fair
to be the object of her simple stare
the playing cards were already there
and his intentions certainly laid bare

the gambler threw the money down
without the faintest form of sound
and tapped his toe gently upon the ground
waiting for the waiter to come around

and bring his gin and tonic

how do you do, he simply asked
her face remained a pretty mask
and so he smiled a smile that basked
in the complication of this task

and sipped his gin and tonic

they played and flirted from he to she
they played and won from she to he

and so the time had come for chivalry
to require him to return her fee

she smiled at the gesture warm and true
"this i cannot permit you to do"
she said as she stood and slowly drew
her tongue across her lips and blew

a simple kiss

i'd prefer your gin and tonic

13.

she wore the dress I'd sewn for her
and wore the look I'd shown to her
and when I was alone with her
my mind flew out the window.

 I sang the song she sang to me
but sang a different melody
and when the song was through with me
her smile became my halo.

and through the smoke
of purity's toke
I saw a heart that once was broke
but fixed itself with rum and coke
and a healthy dose of me.

and through the veil
of heaven and hell
her touch touched me and touched me well
and I continually fell
for her.

14.

She set fire to reality
and soon the ashes covered me.
Through the haze
I saw her gaze
at truths within my earliest days
and I couldn't resist the subtle ways
she soon set my life ablaze.

How could I react in time
... respond to her warm hand in mine,
or say the words I couldn't find
to convey
the way
she held my decay
at bay?

Around my head
revolved thoughts once dead
drenched within a soup of sin and hopes unsaid.

Around my heart
draped the blanket of part

of her, the start
of her, the ups and downs
and smiles and frowns
of her.

I cried aloud
at sky and cloud
and grasped at air
and everywhere
to find a hold
on the solid gold
of the only treasure
I was ever sure
of:
her.

15.

One day
I lay
upon my back, the grass: a warm soft bed.
The sun
did run
across the sky, both hands beneath my head.

The breeze
sang sweetly through the trees
before it kissed my skin.
I traced her face into the clouds, to see her smile
again.

Memories filled my thirsty mind and daydreams fed
my heart.
And everything she left behind keeps her near when
we're apart.

16.

The symphony
of what I see
whenever she
is near to me
reminds me of the song of love
she sang below the dark above
her innocent and peaceful night
when I first caught the simple sight
of flesh and spiritual delight,
when I and she
finally became we.

17.

my life is a paddle boat in the midst of the sea
and there's a storm around this boat of me
wherever i hold my compass the arrow spins
so fast with no way to know which way begins
the way i should go or which way i should try
to find the peace where land meets sky

but you came down from somewhere far
beyond the place where my daydreams are
and calmed the storms of uncertainty
threatening to drown this boat of me
calming words and soothing tones
the peace of love nourishing my bones

wherever did you spend your days
before you showed me all the ways
you knew how to please my mind
where to search and where to find
the love within the very deep of me
now covering all our insecurity

as i rest calm upon the waters
blissfully ignorant of all the others
still struggling to decipher
who to live and who to die for
i am certain within my heart's oath
concerning you, the answer is both

18.

i like the night because it's dark not bright
and i can see the nothing that can't see me.
i like the black because it's light it lacks
and shadows show what i don't know
that i don't know.

so know the moon can't come too soon;
when the sun finally sets my mind suddenly forgets
the entire day and runs away from everything that i
won't say.
i close my eyes underneath the dark skies.
i close my eyes.

you're an evening star, pure and white, at war
with the peace of the late hour - a being of
extraordinary power
fighting effortlessly against the doubt that's at war
with me.
you're the one that i'll let within places where i keep
the light from entering in.
i'll let you in.

say you'll never go away, say that you are here to
stay.
to stay.
say you'll take my offered hand and give to me a soft
command
 to lift you into a life of joy i never knew i never went
to
before i knew a girl like you could light my night the
way you do.
the way you do.

no one lights my night the way you do.

19.

something within her
made something within me
begin to descend to the end
of a dream

and something about her
made living without her
hurt dully and sully the day rather fully
devoid of her contact

so whenever my heart suffers enough to scream
i picture her face and my fantasies react

20.

once there was a time when
i found myself stuck within
a place that i cannot begin
to adequately describe

this place was full of solitude
where light was dark and joy was rude
my heart was thin for lack of food
to feed the need inside

then you appeared from somewhere new
and showed me love i never knew
could build me into someone true
enough to conquer sorrow

and now each day i live in peace
resulting from the daily feast
of love which tames the fickle beast
of longing for tomorrow

i stand content with who i am

where i go and where i stand
determined to ever be your man
we'll go where joy will follow

i rest content with who you are
where you dream, be it near or far
for mine's the night around your star
and love the nourishment we swallow

21.

i fell asleep without a dream
but found one in a memory
reminding me of what i felt
before you fixed my heart

and in this dream, i dreamed a dream
which placed the fleeting temporary
joy of first infatuation
upon foundations permanent

please dream with me this dream i dream
we'll pass the past of solitary
living towards a new elation
born from love's intent

and our life will seem to reflect this dream
contentment builds the sanctuary
where knees of doubt had never knelt
our love become true art

22.

the happiness they wear upon their faces
feels to my eyes like a memory
of something i used to believe
was true

the songs i hear on the radio
feel to my ears like a fantasy
of something i want to believe
is you

i walk down the street
numb to my feet
the wind and the sun fail to register

i look at my hands
absent demands
to experience what reality delivers

the clouds in the sky twist and redefine
their shapes into moments of fancy

the leaves on the trees move and dance in time
to the rhythm of my heart and romance me

the touch of the cloth i wear upon my form
feels to my skin like insanity
or something i try to believe
is true

the taste on my tongue resting still in my mouth
feels to my soul like something lovely
or something i wish to believe
is you

The First Romance

He stood on the horizon where Time parts from
Space, marveling at the cold and the dark. He was a
bright being and inherently warm. Steam covered his
body like a robe. The frigid nothingness struggled
vainly to bite at his still, straight form. It was naught
to him.

His eyes searched the Hemisphere of Time for hope.
They searched the Hemisphere of Space for home.
They searched for what he did not know and they
searched for what he knew he needed.

He did not know the passage of days. Years and eons
were meaningless to him. He felt no self-pity for his
condition. He felt no doubt. He felt no sorrow and no
loss. He had never possessed anything. There was
nothing to lose. Indeed, he did not know what it
meant to possess something. He only knew standing -
standing and searching.

A speck of flame (so small it could be a trick of the eye) stood still upon the furthest reaches of the Hemisphere of Time. He saw it. He thought he saw it. Within him was birthed the first new things: curiosity, but also caution.

The speck of flame grew brighter. It did not stand still. But, even as it moved, it did not do so haphazardly. It moved with purpose towards him. He was an aspiration. His heart felt something newer and more exotic than either curiosity or caution. His heart felt inside-out. He wondered if his aspiration and the speck of flame's aspiration were the same.

She smoldered. She wore fire like a gown and heat like a tiara. Her eyes: two lit coals of certainty. She spoke to him in loud, triumphant song.

"I have found my goal."

"Your goal?"

"You."

"Why am I your goal?"

"Because I need another."

"Any other?"

"No. You. There is no other."

"Why do you need me?"

"My fires are hot and my furnaces powerful. I have no one to share them with. I yearn."

"I will share your fires. Will you share my light?"

"I will share your light."

"My name is Source. What is your name?"

"I am Nameless."

"You are Nameless no longer. You are Hope."

They stood still on the horizon where Time parts from Space and marveled at each other. He did not pay attention to the Hemisphere of Time any longer. He had found hope. He had also found courage.

"Hope, will you come with me?"

"Where will we go?"

"We will search the Hemisphere of Space for something I want us to possess."

"Is it wonderful?"

"I hope it will be very wonderful. I want to search for Home."

They traveled marvelously. A rainbow of light and flame shooting through the cold dark of space. Two arrows of power cutting through nothing. Two arrows of purpose cutting towards something.

A sphere of dust and ash.

It rested within space like a ball in deep water, intriguing the young perspective within their old minds.

"Source, is this Home?"

"Let us see."

They moved through the walls like masters of matter and found a palace of crystal and glass.

Her flame set fire to the dust and the ash. His light burst from the crystal and glass.

"We are home, my Hope."

"We are home, my Source."

The Star burst upon the darkness of nothing like a thunderclap across a still sky...

...housing within it a Romance both new and timeless.

23.

i'm at the crossroads of east and west
in search of she who loves me best
unsure of how to pass the test
of where to find my lover's rest

i'm at the crossroads of north and south
desiring a taste of my lover's mouth
intoxicated as every youth
inebriated by true love's truth

i'm at the crossroads of day and night
in search of she who brings me light
leaving the others to fly their kites
so we can discover each other's delights

i'm at the crossroads of near and far
desiring the knowledge of where you are
and there's no compass nor evening star
to tell me the right direction
there's no map or message in a jar
that'll guide me to your perfection

24.

my reflection doesn't blink at me when i look it in the
eyes
my reflection doesn't copy me when i put on my
disguise
my reflection doesn't smile at me when i mask my
reality
my reflection doesn't hide from my emotional
instability

i search for cracks within reflected composure
i search for hope within reflected postures
i search for healing within reflected sutures
i search for certainty within reflected closure

my reflection will not accompany me when i leave
reality behind
my reflection will not come for me when i find who's
on my mind
my reflection is just a ghost i see when i need a face
that's kind

and since you're far away from me, my reflection
must do fine

25.

sometimes i feel what i don't know how
and think of things i cannot define
sometimes i feel what i can't show how
and think of things i cannot refine
sometimes i feel what i did before
and think of what i said one time
sometimes i feel what i had in store
and think of lives i led one time
sometimes i feel what i thought was forgotten
and think of things i've yet to forget
sometimes i feel what i thought you'd begotten
and think of things i've yet to beget
sometimes i feel what i cannot describe
and think of things unfamiliar
sometimes i feel what i will not abide
and think of things dissimilar
sometimes i feel i think too much
sometimes i think i feel too much
sometimes my rest is restless
sometimes my rest is restless

26.

i'm caught up in a blanket of sunshine
and it tangles my limbs and warms my mind
and i suffocate in the bliss within this vice of mine
an embrace of my face by your love divine
an embrace of my face by your presence
and the fact of your presence being so very fine

i'm caught up in a storm of calm and peaceful
thunder
and it shocks me with the lightning of wonder
and i fly where the tornado casts me asunder
a destruction that takes my most foolish blunder
a destruction that takes my heart
and the fact of my heart - the treasure you plunder

hit me with your words so soft
scratch me with your claws so soft
so deep with your touch so soft
cut me deep with your words so soft

i'm trapped within your prison of liberty

and it tortures the misery i used to be
and i feel the most distant sympathy
for the me my mirror used to see
for the me my mirror used to suffer
and the fact of my suffering is a story you threw
behind me

dig your mind within my soul
tear me up and make me whole
dig your heart within my soul
devour my being until i'm completely whole

i think i might have been a miscreant of confusion
i think i might have been a miscreant of delusion
thank you for your solution
thank you for your solution

so i dream
so i dream so heavy about a love so light
and i dream so heavy about a girl so bright
so i dream
baby, how deeply i dream of you
how very deeply i dream of you

27.

i'm looking at a mural i haven't finished painting
and the colors hit my eyes and send my mind to
fainting
then the unconsciousness covers my dreams like
moonlight
and illuminates the hidden portions of all that's ever
been right
in me
and your eyes are the eyes i see
looking back at me
i see your eyes looking back at me

i'm listening to a song i haven't finished singing
and the melody hits my ears and sends my heart
wringing
then the water from my washrag heart washes like
purity
and cleanses the hidden portions of all that's ever
been dirty
in me
and your eyes are the eyes i see

looking back at me
i see your eyes looking back at me

touch my face with just a finger
just a finger of that soft hand
and know within this husk is the soul of your man

touch my face with just the linger
just the linger of your warm eyes and
know within this husk is the beating heart of your
man

i'm touching a memory i haven't finished creating
and the facts are blurring and the substance deflating
then the details sift through my hands like soft silt
and i'm left with a dagger buried up to its hilt
in me
and your eyes are the eyes i see
looking back at me
i see your eyes looking back at me

your eyes are gentle and your words are warm
as your touch so gentle and your hands so warm
remove the dagger as if it were merely a thorn
and the memory becomes a daydream reborn

touch my face with just a finger...

28.

her eyes bit my face like ice in a storm
her words gripped my heart like a predator's bite
her lips created smiles that took the form
of promises whispered and the lovely sight
of certainty pulled from the midst of what might
happen between the two of us
to join together the two of us

her hair engulfed my face like the sea
her words gripped my soul like destiny
her lips created smiles that seemed to be
created within her heart just for me

her kiss bit my face like morning dew
her words gripped my mind like a daydream
her lips created smiles that said 'i love you'
and everything seemed to me to seem
to be certainties pulled from the steam
generated between the two of us
joining together the two of us

29.

i'm tired of life and bored with days
the nights are dead and all the ways
i used to live are old to me

i want to quit it all and go
somewhere where no one knows
what to make of me

i want to be by myself

i'm tired of hope and bored with trying
love is empty and joy is flying
away with the old dreams

i want to quit it all and leave
behind everything that i believe
so there's nothing to make of me

i want to be by myself

30.

the rainstorm dancing on my roof moves to its own
beat
while the thoughts in my head circle on repeat
and as the moral victory gets pulled from the defeat
my perspective grows where past and future meet

but even when my mind tries to focus on everything
everybody tells me is important
you remain the best, the happiest, the only thing
my body tells me is important

31.

my mind operates on a wavelength that is difficult to
measure
and my heart operates in a storm that is difficult to
weather
emotion complicates life's forecast and like a feather
thrown through maelstroms and the erasure
of all peace
i often tear

i won't require you to calm the winds that beat upon
my days
i don't desire you to sacrifice your energy for me
emotion complicates life's daily trajectory
thrown through a rainbow like a bullet of grays
ending peace
i often fear

if i bleed
my blood runs true
and if i bleed
my blood runs to you

but if i bleed
it's not to die
and if i bleed
the reason why
is there's no tears left to cry

there's just so much goddamned frustration crowding
my brain
and my thoughts operate with a language too alien
emotion complicates my attempts to purge and drain
away the consequences of passions salient
and all peace
is often lost

nerves are raw and skin is naked to eyes uncaring and
distant
and my thoughts operate in a room undecorated
emotion complicates my efforts to transplant
the consequences of passions unrequited
and all peace
bears high costs

if i bleed
my blood will eventually dry

32.

if the sea could catch you up
bring you to me
should we leave the motor behind
and let the sea take us wherever it wanted?
should we let the boat
float
wherever it wound up going?

i don't know if i want control
over my emotions
i don't know if i want control
over what i feel for you.
i think i enjoy the haphazard rhythm
of a heartbeat unsure of what to do with itself.
i think i enjoy the chaos within me when you inject
yourself
into my solid days.
i think i enjoy the storm you create within my mind
whenever my solid days become routine.

if the wind could catch you up

bring you to me
should we leave the wings behind
and let the wind take us wherever it wanted?
should we let our bodies fly
on the breeze
wherever we wound up going?

i want to live surprises with you.
i want to live so many surprises with you.

33.

music is a good language
because it speaks words without diction
and separates the heart's truth
from reality's fiction

music is a good language
because it cuts out the middle man
and nothing explains hope better than
a melody
free
of preconceived notions

music is a good language
because it tells the dream everything
the tongue can't decipher
because it tells the hope nothing
that love won't die for
because it tells my heart
you'll never be apart
from me

and that's the only song i really want to hear.

Do Not Hazard Those Stormy Seas

The moon cast him a disinterested gaze.

He stood on a beach, looking. The storms erupted upon the horizon. The sea danced a seizure of horrifying motions. The wind sang a cacophony of anguished fury.

His young eyes shone with the curious hunger for excitement. They betrayed an absence of fear. They betrayed the hope of inexperience.

The old fisherman recognized what he saw. He smiled in spite of himself.

"Do not hazard those stormy seas, my lad," his ancient voice growled. The old man's vocal chords thrust the sounds from his throat with a grating thud - as if he had spent the better part of his years gargling hot asphalt. His inner scars carved emotion into his words, powerfully. His physical scars carved impressions in the young man's mind - impressions of former glory. Impressions of former loss.

The old man spoke the wisdom of fear. He wore the honesty of that emotion without shame.

"Beyond that horizon, there dwells the Siren," the old fisherman stated with a smack of his chapped lips. It almost sounded like condemnation.

The youth looked past the tumult on the horizon and saw only adventure. He saw promise. He saw escape and release.

"I do not fear your monsters," he replied with a confidence age rarely remembers.

"You should. For they most certainly do not fear you," the old fisherman spat. His mouth wore a smirk but his eyes were cold. They were painted with the glare of doom.

"A little risk never hurt anyone...much..." the young man replied with a silly smile. He tossed his blond hair out of his eyes. It danced in the wind. His hands were not the hands of the timid. They were rough, in spite of his youth. They had worked. They knew toil. Muscle corded his arms and legs. A barrel chest moved easily with the calm breathing of a spirit fully comfortable with the ability of the flesh that clothed it.

The old fisherman saw strength, power and potential. He also saw a fool.

"Do you know what the Siren does, my lad?" he almost whispered. The note of resignation melted into the surrounding storm.

"She sings," the youth whispered in response.

"She does more than that, laddy. She woos," the ancient mariner hobbled closer. "Her song ensnares you by the soul with the claws of hope and longing for comfort that cannot be. Hers is a song that cannot be resisted. Hers is a melody that cannot be fought. If you hear but a note of it, your doom is assured."

The youth looked past the tumult on the horizon and saw only adventure.

"My doom is assured, you say?"

The young man stood straight. He faced the old fisherman. He appeared at peace: certain.

"My doom is assured," he stated.

"Yes," the old man replied, knowing he did not need to do so.

The young man set sail that very evening.

The storm beat upon his tiny ship. He drank in the thrill of fear and felt the rush of the conqueror. He would find things and he would discover places no one knew existed. Or, he would die a spectacular death trying. A silent death. A lonely death. He would die unknown, unsung, unremembered. He smiled at his apathy.

The storm did not relent. The waves cursed his courage and spat at his resolve. However, neither the storm nor the waves could resist the movement of time. The worst of it passed slowly by and the dawn began to peek from under the covers of disaster.

Ever so faintly, the wind teased him with the half-remembered tune of a long-forgotten dream. It invigorated him and he worked his little vessel ever more purposefully towards the horizon. The sun began to paint. The clouds looked more beautiful than they had ever before appeared.

How gently the tune increased its volume. How pleasantly it wrapped his mind up within the blankets and quilts of relief. How softly his thoughts laid themselves down upon the mattress of his mind.

His eyes fixed upon a sight that should have startled him. He viewed a young woman sitting alone upon a rock jutting up from the sea. She sat naked and bold. Her eyes embraced his own.

She was more radiant than any woman he had ever seen.

Her hair was an exotic braid of gold and seaweed. Her eyes were so crystal blue the sea was dull in comparison. Her lips were vivid aquamarine. Her skin was as sea foam and her body was bare and incredible. And, she sang.

Oh, how her song stabbed his soul: how it pierced him. He was home and he was in agony: an agony of longing - like the longing for bed after an exhausting journey. Yes. Yes. He must crawl into bed. He must crawl into a bed of sand and pull the sheets of the sea up over his head.

But, he didn't want to sleep. He wanted her. He didn't want her for her song. He didn't want her for her sex. He wanted her for the adventure and the mystery he saw bursting from her eyes. He wanted her for the doubt he saw behind that adventure and that mystery.

And so he accomplished what no man before had ever done.

He stood up in his boat, looked the Siren in her startled eyes and posed the first question she had ever heard from the mouth of man.

"Are you the Siren?"

She was amazed. Men didn't speak to her. Men silently drowned themselves for her. Oh, but his voice. She liked it. His voice was kind. She was surprised that she liked how kind it was.

"Yes," she whispered in bewilderment.

Her answer was more puzzled than confident. She was still unconquerably confused.

"Will you drown me?" he asked. His voice sang without fear! It was so beautiful. Pure.

The Siren thought that he must suffer for his purity. How dare he show her purity and kindness? The liar.

"Yes," she stated coldly. Her eyes became curtains.

"Why?" he asked. His voice still sang.

She thought he must be mocking her. How could this be honest? It must be an act. How dare he?

"The suffering of men provides me with great pleasure," she said, as she savored each evil word. The cruelty in her voice satisfied her greatly.

"Why?" he asked. His voice still sang. No. It whispered a tune of concern. Her throat clenched and she had difficulty swallowing.

"...I do not wish to say..." she replied hesitantly. The curtains had been torn from her eyes. Her brow was furrowed.

"May I offer something in exchange for my life?" he asked her so sweetly. So kindly. So full of concern.

No! She thought this all must be a lie. A horrible lie! But, what if something is different? What if something is very different right now? Could she take that chance? What harm was there in listening a bit more to his sweet voice? What harm was there in looking at his beautiful blue eyes? They looked like the sky on a clear day. They looked like hope.

"I will hear your offer," she whispered. Her voice carried cruelty no longer.

"I offer you my heart." His statement was so simple and plain it took the Siren a minute to decipher what he had offered.

"What do you mean...?" she started.

"I offer to love you," he interjected immediately.

"You cannot make such an offer!" She wanted to scream it, but it came out as a whimper.

"My heart is my own," he replied. "It is mine to give to whom I wish. I wish to give it to you."

"You are still under the spell of my voice," the Siren said. She felt this must be the case. He could not mean what he had said. These things do not happen. "You do not understand that which you propose."

"No, ma'am. If I was under the spell of your voice, I'd be drowned. I wanted to drown myself. Desperately so, but then I had a realization; and upon having that realization, I no longer had any desire to drown myself." His smile captivated her.

"What was this realization?" she asked. Her voice was so soft now.

"I realized why I set sail," he stated.

"Why did you set sail?" she asked, still very softly.

"To die," he replied. "You see...I had lost faith in life. My betrothed had attempted to use me. She wanted to break off our engagement, but keep me by her side as a failsafe while she looked for a more attractive option. My employer committed fraud against his workers and robbed us of our livelihoods. Everywhere I looked I saw despair. I saw arrogance. I saw selfishness. I saw suffering. I saw evil. I sought adventure so that I might embrace death wearing a smile - having attempted to conquer a mighty challenge. I had lost faith in life because I had lost faith in ever finding goodness, truth... or love." His eyes smiled at her as broadly as his lips.

"...you cannot say that you love me..." she murmured as her head shook with disbelief.

"But, I do," he replied. His voice overflowed with kindness and warmth.

"You do not know me! I am a spirit of the sea and I seek the doom of men!" she shouted. Her voice had regained its volume, but not its prior violence.

"No. You are a woman who is alone and you seek comfort," he responded with a gentle firmness.

"I need no comfort!" Her dismissal was angry, but it carried no weight of conviction or certainty.

"Why, then, do you sing of it?" he asked.

"...what...?"

Where had her voice gone? It had become a hushed echo.

"...what...?"

"Your song? It is a ballad of longing," he said. His voice gained strength in his certainty. "You yearn for comfort. You need it so desperately you cannot help but sing that enchanted tune. It drives men crazy with longing - so insane they kill themselves...because you cannot die yourself...you seek to heal your wound with the wounds of others. I want to heal your wound with love."

"...no...I..." This was all too much. She could no longer pretend to possess even the most basic control over her emotions. Her eyes darted everywhere. Everywhere. As long as they didn't look at this man. They couldn't look at this man.

"I want to love you," he said. "I want to give you that which you need. I want to give you myself."

"...I..." Her head was swimming. Her heart was racing. Her mouth was dry.

"May I love you?" he asked.

He stepped out of the boat and waded through the shallow water towards the rock upon which she sat. He climbed the rock and stood facing her, looking deep within her crystal eyes. He saw the tears of truth that rested on her enchanted cheeks and the doubt behind the adventure and the mystery was now intermingled with a glimmer of hope.

"May I love you?" he asked again.

His whispered question carried sweetness so very gently.

Her eyes closed. She sobbed.

He took her pale face into his hands. Her skin was cold to his touch. Her eyes opened to him and tears ran down her cheeks.

He kissed her.

And the Curse of the Siren was broken by a man who was broken by doubt.

And the life of that man was saved by she who had sought to snuff it out.

34.

i rise from bed and my empty head
becomes filled with you and love instead
of that old solitary dread
of a new day cold and old life dead

i walk outside where night has died
and feel the breath enter inside
these tired lungs that tried
to get by without your sky by my sun's side

surround my flesh with your embrace
profound your touch upon my face
confound my doubt whenever you trace
the sound of your voice in the shape of love's grace

i dance within a room that's bare
and move towards your pleasant stare
eyes beckoning mine to please play fair
to romance your dance with subtle flair

pull the cover of life over both of us

dull the blade of the knife separating us
cull the joy from the strife of reality
full of the hope of you with me
i want to be
full of the hope of you with me

35.

storms brewing in your eyes tell me stories
reveal secrets and warn me of mysteries
pain strikes like lightning
doubt rolls like thunder
storms brewing in your eyes tell me worries

your silent mouth is closed and peaceful
your distant expression is most deceitful
your tears fall like snow
they cover the ground below
in quiet suffering i cannot know
because you won't show
me what exists behind the curtain of your mind

36.

take some time
talk it out
take some time
breathe without
taking time
to think about
everything
you live without
everything
you dream about

look around
drink it in
look around
take it in
look around
where i begin
looking around
for where it ends
all around
potential love and potential sin

surrounding all of you within
all of me
all of you within
all of me
surrounding all of you within
all of me

hearts full of fantastic maybes

37.

i sit at the edge of reality
and fantasy takes a peek at me
as if it sees what i see
whenever i see your beauty

my eyes blinking
my mind thinking
my thirsty soul begins drinking
your words
and daydreams begin sinking
within your voice unheard

i sit at the edge of typical days
and evenings take my hours away
as if to say only sleep can weigh
the truths of life no one can say

my eyes blinking
my mind thinking
my thirsty soul begins drinking
your words

and daydreams begin sinking
within your voice unheard

i sit at the edge of reality
i sit at the edge of reality

38.

life shared a glimpse of joy with me
and then, as if to toy with me,
it covered up the joy i see
with a blanket
silently
wrapping up my expectations
and the ship that set sail from my heart
mere moments before
life sank it
silently
wrapping up my expectations
in the sea of the unknown tomorrow
mere moments before
i could thank it
for giving me
even one glimpse
of you

even one glimpse,
and not one more since,
of you...

39.

once upon a time, a boy held out his hand
and asked of Life to help him grasp and help him
understand
why joy and sadness made him cry
when hello was so strong an opposite to good-bye

why did laughter sound like sobbing
when the passion of each gave way to throbbing
physical motions and cratered emotions
like hurricanes without an ocean
as if the night possessed brighter light that the moon
was simply robbing

help me, please, to comprehend
the boy asked quietly of the Wind
why does cold hurt like heat
and why does my heart more quickly beat
whenever fear bids me retreat
or love bids me repeat
words i've never heard before
until beauty's face opens the door

that held them tight
and out of sight
within the shadows within my mind
why does my heart more quickly beat
to stand still in love or run in fear of defeat
why is my soul blind
to explanations of this kind

i want to know why my mouth grows dry
when i see her smile or hear her sigh
i want to know why my tired eye
snaps open the instant she saunters by
i want to know why my tongue once shy
starts singing songs and speaking highs
starts whispering love and painting skies
with dreams of hope and an absence of lies
surrounding two souls weary of so many good-byes

i've lived a life of too many good-byes
these days have been days of too many good-byes
please tell me, Life...
i want to know why

40.

the sun wounds my atmosphere with blades of light
piercing my dream with the pain of waking
but, when the day introduces your face to my sight
my lungs find it difficult to continue taking
breaths of air

the moon pierces my atmosphere with knives of night
wounding my dream with the pain of longing
but, when rapid-eye movement introduces your
delight
my lungs find it difficult to continue belonging
with the air

my life is injured every now and then
scabs and sores sometimes begin
distracting my focus until i see
your smiling eyes looking back at me
your smiling eyes looking back at me

41.

sunlight beats upon my brow,
each step feels like a struggle.
exhausted thoughts forgetting how
to think beyond my troubles.
perspiration coats my skin;
the dryness in my mouth begins
to ask me for relief again:
for just one drink of water.

humidity and heat desire to
join together and conspire to
transform all that i admire to
something quite uncommon.

heartbeats slow and breathing races
yours rises o'er a sea of faces:
my soul forgets where its place is
among the frivolous or solemn.

reality beats upon my life,
each hour feels like a struggle.

exhausted dreams bored with strife,
disinterested in troubles.
perspiration coats my skin;
the dryness in my mouth begins
to ask me for relief again:
for just one drink of water.

42.

i search without looking, wondering like a random
note
where my place is among this song.
i walk without direction, wandering like a random
boat
upon a sea with nothing on the horizon.

you can provide me with a goal if you desire
yours is better than nothing I suppose
or we can ignore responsibility and fire
warning shots in the air for those
that think doing things their way
is the only way to do things the right way

i don't know what i want
besides knowing i want your hand in mine
besides knowing i want your smile to find
mine

i don't know what i want
besides knowing i want your dream beside mine

besides knowing i want your eyes to find
mine

i'll make us drinks and we can sit and watch night
rebel against the day
let's invest our time in wasteful ways and watch night
rebel against the day

43.

comfort eludes me
i can't find peace
dreaming deludes me
my worry won't cease
and, i know better
than to burden myself with the future
i know better
than to burden myself with the future
but, i'm unsure
how to stop

do i prefer dark or light
i can't get warm
do i prefer day or night
this worry's a storm
and, i know better
than to burden myself with life
i know better
than to burden myself with life
but, the strife
won't stop

i'm looking for certainty
when i know it's a luxury
i can't afford

i'm looking for a purpose crystalline
when i know it's a routine
i can't afford

my hands are in my pockets
holding tight to air and silence
my eyes are in their sockets
holding tight to your presence
and, when i walk there's a solace
contained within each heavy moment
and, so i walk where your face
clouds my vision, and each breath spent
living is a breath spent for you
each breath spent living is a breath spent for you

44.

the morning arrives
and the bright hits my eyes
with the knowledge that I must awake

but, then my mind finds your face
in a most pleasant place
where my reality these daydreams forsake

we talk and we touch
and there is so much
between us that brings to us joy

these daydreams are fine
because dreams of this kind
responsibilities cannot destroy

your eyes glimmer and tease
and your body's curves please
every nerve and synapse in my mind

these daydreams are fine
because dreams of this kind
leave all this reality behind

your beauty designs
every dream of this kind
and I leave my reality behind

I leave all my reality behind

He Had Never Felt the Rain

A man sat on a bench. It rained upon him. He sat dry.

He had never felt the rain. An invisible bubble of unknowable force surrounded him. It always had. His skin had never felt the warm showers of summer or the cold pelt of winter. He envied his friends. They wondered why. After all, he never needed an umbrella. Wasn't that a blessing?

He sat on the bench, looking at the lake. The grey sky sneered at the earth. The green, lush grass mocked the atmosphere with indifference. The downpour chilled the air. Huddled forms scurried for shelter. Even the birds struggled to find refuge together among the branches of trees. He watched the drops hit the water. He marveled at each tiny cascade. He sat dry in a storm.

She had never felt the sun. A small cloud hovered over her. It always had. Her skin had never felt the warm embrace of summer light or the cold touch of the winter breezes. She envied her friends. They wondered why. After all, she never needed to worry about sunburn. Wasn't that a blessing?

She sat on a bench, looking at the lake. The blue sky smiled at the earth. The green, lush grass laughed with the atmosphere at an inside joke. The light warmed the air. Carefree children danced around in the grass near the lake and played, and sang, and threw giggles at the air while their parents sat pleasantly and smiled comfortably. She watched the birds fly in the heavens. She marveled at their beauty. She sat soaked on a bright summer day.

He walked down the sidewalk towards the park.

She walked down the sidewalk towards the park.

He thought about life and what it meant to live in a bubble.

She thought about life and what it meant to live under a cloud.

He thought about the future and what it meant to feel only dryness.

She thought about the future and what it meant to feel only discomfort.

He ran into her running into him.

"Excuse me," he said as he averted his eyes in embarrassment at his carelessness.

"I'm so sorry," she said as she struggled to straighten her dress and appear as dry and normal as her drenched form would permit.

Their eyes soon met and something was communicated. A very particular something carrying a great deal of meaning joined his mind with hers and hers with his.

Their mouths both opened slightly and then closed again quite quickly since each found an immediate need to swallow.

They understood they had reached a crossroads.

The unknown looked into their eyes.

Was this safe? Was the other safe? Was familiarity preferable to understanding?

He reached up, purposefully, and began to wipe the rain from her cheek.

The cloud struck him fiercely with its lightning.

He ignored it.

He reached with his other hand, purposefully, and wiped the tear from her other cheek.

The cloud struck him violently with its lightning.

His bubble burst.

The incomprehensible cloud pierced the unknowable force surrounding him.

A breath of warmth embraced her face like the smile of an old friend nearly forgotten and just now reunited.

A mist of storm kissed his cheek with the tenderness of a grandmother's touch.

She looked up and saw his sun. She felt the rays upon her smile.

"How did this happen?" Her voice cracked with that sweet combination of sobbing and laughter - the kind that occurs when joy does not know if it really has a right to be joy.

"I made it happen," he replied. The words left his mouth before he understood why he said them.

"How did you make this happen?"

"By risking everything I knew for someone I didn't."

He knew. He knew with a certainty that rivaled gravity itself. The knowledge gave him a foundation to stand upon. He planted his feet firmly upon this foundation.

She noticed when he did so and asked him, "Why did you do this?"

"Because it felt ... right."

He looked up and saw the rain. He felt the drops hit his smile.

"Thank you," he told her honestly.

"Why are you thanking me? I have done nothing," she admitted simply.

"You have shared yourself with me."

"I didn't even know that's what I was doing."

"That doesn't matter. You shared yourself with me and now I understand."

They kissed.

And for the rest of their days they lived with a cloud that only rained when desired and a sun that always shined when required.

And their friends wondered how it all had happened.

Wasn't it a blessing?

45.

i am thinking
like she's drinking -
casually

and my thoughts
they get caught
casually

within each swirl
of the straw of my girl
casually

stirring

i am thinking about
living without
casually

ignoring everyone
as i've done
casually

from the beginning
and i watch her straw spinning
casually

i am regarding her face
and recalling the place
casually

where we met for the first
and now my expectations burst
casually

during

this evening's respite
this evening's respite

46.

I was just going through the motions
but, then you entered in
my life and when
I found you I also found emotion

I don't doubt for a single moment
that everything makes sense
since you hopped my fence
you bettered my life in an instant

even though
sometimes I don't know
where to start

I know you're there
and that you'll share
your comfortable heart

I was just going through the motions
but, then you introduced
yourself, and seduced
that part of me that forgot emotion

I will not hesitate to say
that everything makes sense
since you hopped my fence
and became the best part of my every day

the rough places don't hurt as much
since I gained your touch

the rough places don't hurt so much
now I've gained your touch

47.

if home is where the heart is
how can my heart run away with you?
can my heart run away?
can it get away from all that's here?
can it retire from expectations,
from daily realizations
that apparent certainty stands hours away
from tomorrow becoming today
and muddying yesterday's clear
water?
i bought her time...
thought her mine.
but, years bring more than age -
perspective colors my daily wage
with more potent colors than cash.
she's not mine
and i'm fine
not being hers
but...freedom is a complicating
issue captivating
more than the affection of my attention...

freedom means letting go
when passion forces yes to no
and open hands to fists closed...

if home is where the heart is
how can my heart run away with you?
does home become a contradiction?
will clever diction
circumvent conviction?
will wit and measure
dull a treasure
so used to pleasure
the nerves are bored?
i don't know what to do sometimes
but i feel what's right
because what's right holds tight
to my imagination
and brings satisfaction
to not giving in
when
all i want to give in to
is everything worth giving in to
you
and there's a lot within you
worth giving in to...

i might begin to
think of feeling you
but this is all i'll hold on to...
because the unintended consequences
of thoughts are less expensive
than the price of refunding a restive me
to prior conceptions of proper reality.

if home is where the heart is
may i live in a dream?
may i mute reality's white noise
and be the very best of boys
within my homey illusion...?
why did playing pretend
ever have to end
when playing pretend
sends
smiles to shadows
and cold hands to warm pockets...?

48.

I'm looking for a theme
I need a theme to paint my day
a focus for my eyes at play
to keep my mind in order
a focus for my work today
to keep my mind in order

Life is only tedious if I permit it to be
and a theme will cover me well
a light to drown the dark of apathy
a warmth to blanket the cold of cynicism
a theme will cover me nicely
and warm is a good thing to be

I may be a man but I'm still a boy
and I like adventures
I may be a man but I'm still a boy
and I want to be heroic
fearless and romantic

I'm looking for a purpose
something more immediate than a goal
a focus for my eyes at play

to keep my mind hand in hand with my soul
a focus for my work today
to keep my imagination off the dole
to keep my spirit off the dole

Once my inspiration becomes a beggar
it'll be too easy to please me
and I don't ever want it to ever be
I don't ever want there to ever be
an easy way to sate the hunger of inspiration within
me

Keep me hungry
Keep me hungry

49.

my blood doesn't want to move
but my heart forces it to flow.
my feet don't want to walk
but my mind forces them to go.
my thoughts don't want to think
but curiosity forces them to know.
my pores don't want to sweat
but doubt sometimes makes it so...

fear can make my mouth taste dry.
anxiety can turn my words into sighs.
reality can take every hello
my insecurity wants her mouth to show
and transform each into another good-bye.
fear can make my mouth taste dry.

my blood doesn't want to move.
the cold is comfortable in a nothing place.
but, she silently forces it to flow,
injecting my cells with the warmth of her face.
and i'll wear holes into the soles of my shoes
walking steadily towards the hope of true

and filling the hole in my soul with something more than spirit...
i want some flesh within it...
i want her flesh within it...

50.

My body lay still and steady
while my mind sat up in my bed
ready
to move
needing to move anywhere
but there
in bed
So, leaving my head
I wandered away from myself
to a better vision of life
where colors are more vivid
there's a prevalence of emotion
devoid of the livid
and strife
I wandered towards images and fleeting glimpses
of comfort and solace
those hidden gremlins that toy with me during
sunlight hours
and the sweets and sours that tease my tongue
now tease my eyes
Oh, the flavors I see match the symphony

of hope
that dopes me up: higher, the epiphanies carry me
higher
the Sky is on fire
but I'm not hot
and I'm not cold
I'm just here, ready to behold
more than I've ever held when awake
Don't shake me!
I like where I am.
My sheets are pleasant and my pillow is my carriage.
Don't shake me!
Don't bring me back, yet.
Not yet.

Not yet.

Not yet.

51.

my heart doesn't have a switch
so i can't turn it off and on when convenient
and the feelings i feel can steal the sentiment
from the moment

my mind gets slapped sometimes
by frustration with whatever situation
variety's feelings pull from imagination
and i get sent

spinning

do you remember when we were young
and being dizzy was nothing but fun
so we'd spin ourselves while facing the sun
and fall on the ground, breathless and done

do you remember?

spinning

my mind gets switched whenever
my heart gets a hold of whatever
shadow my memory forgot to forget
and doubt becomes a drink of regret

and i find myself

spinning

my body can't do what it used to
but who i am can handle what i couldn't before
and there's something frenetic about what's in store
for me when your face is the face i see
through the bedroom window of my illusion of
reality...

forgive me while i start

spinning

forgive me while i spin...

come spin with me
come spin with me
come spin with me...

52.

opportunity
necessarily
takes me by my hand
and leads me to stand
bare before vulnerability

i just might
hide from the sight
of all who don't understand
the who of me or where i am
but the mirror reflects more than light

so should i risk an honest smile
attempt to walk an honest mile
or think about her potential while
bathing in the honest grime of living...?

is it careless to throw words at a pretty ear
pretty words in case she should happen to hear
the things that are easier to say when you fear
no consequences of consequence
or happenstances that happen to introduce
themselves...?

riddles for spare moments
while her beauty presents
itself for my appreciation
i appreciate the presentation
i appreciate the sensation
of spare moments spent virtually
with the glimpses of the girl she
has chosen to reveal...

53.

Regarding my eldest son sleeping
my heart keeps beating and my mind keeps keeping
the memories of my father's father
whose name my eldest son bears
my mind keeps keeping
the memories of my father's father
playing in the background
as I'm regarding my eldest son sleeping

Regarding my eldest son at play
my eyes drink in his smile and all the while
the memories of my grandfather's son
who shares the name of this yellow-haired one
my eyes drink in his smile and all the while
the memories of my grandfather's son
playing in the background
playing in the background
as I'm regarding my eldest son at play

The blood runs plain and true through our veins
the blood of men, flawed but good
the blood of men, flawed but good

Regarding my eldest son learning to be
learning to live by regarding me
and the memories of my father's son
who named this boy
and the memories of my father's son
who named this boy
these memories of innocence and learning
playing in the background
playing in the background
as I'm regarding my eldest son learning
learning
learning to be by regarding me

54.

she moves like nothing else
and woos like something else
within a part
that stands apart
from the rest of the things
the full and empty everythings
within the rest of me

she moves and woos like hope

her bones are pretty like nothing else
their shapes are pretty like something else
within a dream
that rests between
the sheets covering all the things
the full and empty everythings
within the heart of me

her bones are pretty like hope

her eyes are daring like nothing else
they're sharp and dangerous like something else
within the sweat

dripping hot and wet
from my brow, a result of all the things
the full and empty everythings
within the anxiety of me

her eyes inspire like hope

i like watching her move
i like watching her watching me watching her move
because she can see me discovering hope within her

when my eyes are full of her
my eyes are full of hope

when my eyes are full of her
my eyes are full of hope

55.

she's a pale princess
and there's no recess
too deep to scare me away
from diving down
to drown
within the promise
contained within
her milky skin

i'll dream of days
where we can play
each other's games

i'll dream of days
where we're free
to play

she's a pale princess
and there's no congress
sophisticated enough to legislate
my desire away
and there's no magistrate

who'll condemn my desire away
from you
and all you do
to me

i'll dream of days
when we can play
each other's games

i'll dream of nights
when we're free
to play

Because I Want You to be Happy

"Because, I want you to be happy."

"Okay."

And so, I earned my first girlfriend.

I was 15 years old, sitting in the cafeteria of an uninteresting high school. She walked in through the double doors with three friends of hers. She passed in front of me. She wore a smile that gave birth to an emotion I found marvelous. My stomach felt tickled, punched and embraced all at once: chaotic, painful and addicting.

I stood up, walked to her table and sat down next to her. She looked at me, her face curious.

"Hello," I said.

"Hello," she replied hesitantly.

I do not think she hesitated out of uncertainty. I think she hesitated because she found the situation humorous.

"My name is Jonah."

"I'm Heather."

"I want to be your boyfriend."

"Why?"

...

And so, I had earned my first girlfriend.

...

Her lips were warm. It was a warmth that puzzled
while comforting me. All the warmth I had
experienced before was created by something. The
stove, the hearth, the sun – they all warmed me from
without. Her lips bled warmth into me like chicken
soup.

"Thank you for kissing me," she said, simply.

"You're welcome. Did you like it?"

"Kiss me again."

...

I moved effortlessly from being alone to being half of a couple. It was rewarding seeing her smile because of me, simply because I was me. I was learning how to love and what that meant.

…

"Why have you been crying?"

My voice contained the same concern my face wore while asking the question.

"Because, I have to tell you something I don't want to."

"What is it?"

"My dad got a new job in South Dakota. We're moving this weekend. He hired a company to pack up all our stuff. We'll be living in a hotel until we find a house."

"South Dakota."

"Yeah, South Dakota."

"Heather?"

"Yes?"

"I'm glad I have two more days with you."

"Should we do something special?"

"I just want to look at you as much as I can, talk to
you as much as I can, hear you as much as I can… so I
can remember you perfectly, forever."

"Are you as sad as I am?"

"Yes."

…

"Hello?"

"Hi, Jonah. It's me, Heather."

"Hi! How's South Dakota?"

"Cold and boring."

"I'm sorry."

"I miss you."

"I miss you, too. I'm glad you called me. I was
planning on calling you tonight."

"I thought you would. I'm impatient."

…

"Hello?"

"Hi, Jonah. It's me, Heather."

"Hello!"

I wondered if she could hear my smile.

"What's up?"

"A boy in my English class asked me to go with him to the homecoming dance."

I paused for a bit. I knew this time would come eventually. I prepared myself for it. It was time for me to say...

"It took him long enough."

"What?"

"Heather, you're beautiful, kind and fun. Boys are going to be interested in you."

"But…"

"I miss you, Heather. I want you to be with me, but I can't make that happen. We're still kids and we have

133

no real power over our lives right now. I'm not going to try to force you to give up the last two years of high school for a boy hundreds of miles away."

We both permitted a silence of understanding to exist for a few moments.

"Is he nice?" I asked softly.

"What?"

"The boy who asked you out. Is he nice to you?"

"Yes. He's very sweet. And, he's shy. He was blushing the whole time he was talking to me."

"Did you say 'yes' to him?"

Her silence answered my question before her voice replied...

"...yes..."

"Good. I hope you have a lot of fun at the dance."

"Are you hurt?"

"Terribly. I can't control my feelings, Heather. But, I'm not going to let them tell me how to treat you."

"I wish you were taking me to the dance."

"Me, too. But this guy, what's his name?"

"Michael."

"Michael. This guy, Michael. Hopefully, he'll be a lot of fun."

"You hope so?"

"Yes."

"Why?"

"Because, I want you to be happy."

56.

soft hands reach gently within
the depths of this heart
they dodge the fangs and the thorns of all my sin
bravely they delve the depths of this heart

soft hands reach gently within
when they find the callous of my regret
they tear it from that place love's rarely been
from that place of hidden hope that I forget
is there
until her hand is there

she tears it out of me
she rips it like paper
she rips it apart like paper

she tears it out of me
she rips it like paper
she rips it apart like paper

there's a risk inherent for a heart un-walled
the flesh is bare

the palpitations clear for all who stare
warm blood of simple desire pumping where called
so much risk inherent for a heart un-walled

she won't stab me with words unguarded
like others ran me through
words unguarded ran me through
such simple weapons cause sophisticated wounds
their tongues were lashes beating wicked tunes
they ran me through
they ran me through
my sunrise dark before it started

she won't stab me with words unguarded

her touch is soft upon my heart
her fingers move with gentle concern
they comfort the cushion holding each dart
thrown by those with little concern
her fingers soothe each ache and burn
caused by those with little concern
her touch is soft upon my heart

there's a risk inherent for a heart un-walled
the flesh is bare
the palpitations clear for all who stare

warm blood of simple desire pumping where called
so much risk inherent for a heart un-walled

my hidden hope now nourished by her kindness
my hidden hope now visible in my blindness
my hidden hope now held by the silence
my hidden hope now rescued from absence

she keeps it dear
wrapping it up in pretty paper
she wraps it up in pretty paper

she keeps it dear
wrapping it up in pretty paper
she wraps it up in pretty paper

who knew my hope would make a gift her love
would prefer
to more material things
to fancier
more stereotypically romancier things

maybe her words are true
even unguarded
maybe her words are true

57.

standing outside when it's cold
and i'm improperly attired
reintroduces my mind to my nerves

standing alone when i'm told
the proper thing to do is mingle
reintroduces my mind to my nerves

standing in the woods when the spring is new
and birds reacquaint themselves with my ears
their songs reintroduce my mind to peace

standing next to her and i have no clue
how she creates the still thrill within me
and she reintroduces my mind to peace

i dance without moving
and sing without sounding
feeling a joy without definition

she teases and pleases
when her gentle hand squeezes
mine and i have no definition

for her...

58.

the moon insists on looking down on me
a penetrating gaze
reminding me of turbulent nights and spent days
the moon insists on looking down on me
a penetrating eye
reminding me of my mouth dry and your soft thigh
the moon insists
the moon insists on making contact with my vision
lunar light so soft yet lacking the sun's precision
and so my dreams seem clearer by comparison

i get it
i get it
stop looking at me like that
but the moon always gets its way

the moon wins every 24 hour argument
getting the last word when the sun has set
the moon makes sure i can't forget
the way you look when my pillow reintroduces itself
to my face

and your phantom reintroduces your form to the lace
that surrounds your passion and tempts my tongue

if i talk in my sleep, your name will belong among the
throng
of words that knowing ears will hear if near enough
if i talk in my sleep, your description will belong
among the throng
of syllables that impossible possibles throw at me
when i'm sleepy

i get it
i get it
the moon keeps looking at me like that
and the moon keeps looking at me like that
always getting its way

59.

the moonlight was fading
and I was watching her masquerading
as an angel.
I couldn't tell
what my heart was doing inside
my chest or why my eyes could no longer confide
what they honestly beheld
to my curious mind and I felt
overwhelmed
by her dance

an amber hue colors my perspective
I find myself learning how to live
again, how to breathe again
I find myself learning how to live
again, how to be again
I can't drop the weapon she's handed me
it's a simple blade of true liberty.
my spirit is free
and overwhelmed
by her dance

I don't want to think about
not being able to dream about
her

I don't want to silence the shout
that tears itself without
her

I don't want to forget
the sun she sets
in this sky

I don't want to beget
any hint of regret
in her eyes

I want her to overwhelm me some more
I want her to overwhelm me with her amber hue
I want her to overwhelm me with her true
beauty
I want to be

overwhelmed by
her dance

overwhelmed by
her dance

60.

the seed of chaos takes root within the heart of my
quiet places
the germ within this seed is unique
when left dry it grows quick
but, you water it
you water it
you water it with your genuine smile
and the soil of potential keeps the seed at rest
and so the soil of potential keeps the seed at rest
in the heart of my quiet places

you possess the only watering can
that can focus my attention upon truer things
you can focus my attention upon purer things

there's a timeless promise that serves as earth beneath
my feet
there's a timeless promise that serves as air within my
lungs
there's a timeless promise that serves as sun upon my
skin
there's a timeless promise that serves as a light at the

end of my tunnel

but, you

you help me keep my balance by holding my hand
you help me keep my focus by kissing my cheek
you help me keep my joy by sharing your smile
you help me keep my peace by quietly loving

me

you possess a wonderful watering can

water me daily
water me daily

i want to be your hero

i want to slay all the dragons for you

i want to be your hero

but, some days my sword is heavier than usual
some days my sword is heavier than usual
and my reflexes are slower than they need to be

i want to be your hero
do you want me to be your hero?

61.

there was a shadow in the corner of the dream
infecting my mind last evening;
reflecting images of passages of verse rehearsed by
my heart when presented
with possibilities of butterflies feasting upon the
honey of infatuation.

i rested silently in the darkness of the shadow, feeling
the cold relief of evening
upon my skin like ice on a burning man's tongue, my
eyes closed - my spirit presented
with potential shortness of breath: my lungs feasting
upon the oxygen of inspiration.

there was a glimmer in the eye of the face infecting
my mind last evening;
reflecting mystery - a potent secrecy - produced by
your beauty when presented
to my longing: possibilities of goose bumps and the
anticipation of tonight's imagination...

62.

there's a heartbeat i dance to
when i dance with you
in the night

there's a breath i breathe
after the air leaves
me

there's an eye i see
when you see me
looking

there's a gleam within
your grin

there's a dream within
the when
the where
and the there
of us

there's a heartbeat i dance to
when i dance with you
in delight

and the night ignites my mind
with everything i find
everything i discover
about my lover

about you

about the lover
i discovered
in you

63.

there's a simple subtlety
a gentle ingenuity
an innocent gratuity
within the where and when
of the what and how
we show each other
what fun's about

i like the play and runaround
the silly words not quite profound
the flirty phrases that freely abound
within the where and when
of the what and how
we tease each other
what fun's about

so play my game
and i'll play yours
show me
your mysteries
and i'll open doors
within you

no one has opened before
we'll see
what my company
has in store for you
and we'll see
what your company
has in store for me

play my game
and i'll play yours

play my game
and i'll play yours

64.

there's a symphony
in all i see
whenever she
reveals herself to me
and the music that bathes my eyes
injects me with drugs that trip me to highs
but the crash never comes
and the crash never comes
when i'm high on her
and all my dreams rest upon her
like silk on a gown
and insincerity on a frown
the crash never comes
when she gets me high

65.

this woman is so different from me
she's smooth like the fabric of time
she's smooth like the fabric of time
this woman is so inspiring to me
she's smooth like the fabric of time

this woman is so different from me
she smells like the memory of peace
she smells like the memory of peace
this woman is so comforting to me
she smells like the memory of peace

this woman is so different from me
she feels like the silence of night
she feels like the silence of night
this woman is so necessary to me
she feels like the silence of night

this woman is so different from me
she quiets the noise in my life
she quiets the noise in my life
this woman is so calming to me
she quiets the noise in my life

and I sleep more soundly
and I walk more steadily
and I dream more pleasantly
and I smile more easily

because she is present

66.

times in life that command my heart:
Stand.
define my dreams and what my hand
should hold...
...define my days and what my mind
should hold...
define
this mind
of mine

and hours of days present opportunities:
Breathe.
feel the air as it fills the lungs
that hold...
...oxygen that fuels my days and what my mind
should hold...
remind
this mind
of mine

to hold onto you

hold on to you

these dreams are dark in color but not in feeling
the colors richly cover my vision and fill my spirit
like a feast of nourishment
a feast of life

these dreams are dark in color but not in feeling
the colors bring your face to my vision and you fill
my eyes
like a feast of nourishment
a respite from strife

i hold onto you

hold on to you

times in life that command my heart:
Rest.
define my dreams and what my mouth
should say...
...define my days and what my tongue
should say...
define
these words
of mine

and hours of days present opportunities:
Inhale.
the illusion of you fills the hole
that holds...
...promise for passion and the desire of nerves
that hold...
your hand
this man
holds your hand

to hold onto you

hold on to you

67.

your hair tangles within dream and night.
your smile tangles with a wicked delight.
your body carves itself from
dreams I didn't know before
the dreams your beauty showed before
my eyes began to taste the sight
of your illusion within my late delight.

words came tumbling off my daydream tongue.
I climbed your ladder without stepping on the lowest
rung.
your presence killed the weight of my past tense
without shooting your gun.
things I didn't understand before
the camera met your hand before
my eyes began to hear the sound
of your illusion within a song I'd never sung
before…
…but I still knew all the words.

68.

you're a book of many covers
and i don't know which one to judge.

one makes me want to read right away.
one makes me want to stare all day.
one asks me to keep other readers away.
one asks me to carry it around all day.

but, there's another
unlike all the others

this cover

shows me dreams that i can taste
and paints vistas that touch my face -
pours water down my back
and washes me of all i lack.

this cover

tantalizes with promise,
cloaks struggle in a quilt of bliss,
makes molehills of mountains
and refreshment of fountains.

this cover

expands my lungs with breath,
sings a lullaby to Death,
stops a threat with a word
and conveys meaning unheard.

this cover

has helped me discover
there's not another
book I'd rather

read.

69.

There's a face
in the place
disappointment left for me
when promise left me

There's a face
at the end of the race
I ran when all I can see
became all I saw behind me

I don't flee much
I won't flee much
But this is such
a downer
a real tear-drop drowner
that I wouldn't mind hitching a ride
with a driver possessing better fortune inside
the present than my present
presents me

There's a face
in the dark space

shadows conspired to create for me
when doubt's variety ate me

I sit digested
my mind congested
with a cacophony of what might have been
and a lobotomy of everywhere I ever might have been
But, it'll all get better

Even on the worst day, the sun is still a setter
Even on the very worst day, that sun is still a setter

70.

There's a place behind my face
where my dreams pretend they're real
and there's a dream within my heart
pretending that my hands can feel
your skin
pretending that my words are real
within
you

There's a place behind your eyes
where my dreams pretend to hide
and there's a storm that beats within my heart
pretending that it's really inside
a song
pretending that it's voice cried
out long
for you

I walk along the boundary
of what I feel and what I see
knowing that possibility
is different from everything actual

But I smile when I picture you in front of me
smiling your smile illuminatingly
shining on the tapestry imaginary
that hangs on the wall where nothing factual

Exists

I need these dreams
they keep me sane
because they are perfect
within a world
that isn't

71.

On complicated days, your beauty sets me free
to dream of a quieter, simpler existence

and I need these dreams to comfortably
ease reality's stresses that tense

my nerves and expectations
my muscles and reservations
my jaw and the insinuations
of this life

Your beauty covers the sights my closed eyes see
with joy

On complicated days, your smile rescues me
from the tedium of responsibility

and I need these rescues to peacefully
comfort any insecurity

my heart possesses
my mind possesses
my spirit possesses
in this life

Your beauty covers the sights my closed eyes see
with joy

Your beauty covers the sights my closed eyes see
with joy

72.

Sometimes I sit in solitude,
my heart partaking of the food
of silence
and the drink of rest,
nourishing my dreams unconfessed
by my mouth

these dreams are mine
and I do not share them
no one can find
where I hide them
but me

Now I sit in solitude
admitting my heart a bit confused
by silence
and I think of you,
ignorant of who
I truly am

And I want to share
because
of reasons I do not understand

even if you are not always here
to listen

even if you go away tomorrow

I will not regret a single moment
nor a single thought I have spent
focused on you

For reasons I do not understand

He Sat Alone

He sat alone and content. He read. The quiet felt like the company of an old friend. He had always been this way. Always happy within the embrace of solitude. He was never lonely, because he was always content. He was content in public. He was content in private. He awoke each morning content with his life and went to bed each evening content with his day. He longed for nothing and smiled at everything.

She was surrounded by her friends, yet lonely. They talked about things that didn't matter to her. The sounds of their chatter helped numb the loneliness within. She had always been this way. Always empty, in spite of her friends' attention. She was always lonely, because she was never content. There was always something missing... something she couldn't quite put her finger on. She awoke each morning anxious with her life and went to bed each evening nervous about tomorrow. She longed for *something* and rarely smiled.

...

"It means a lot to me that you're coming," his little brother said.

"Of course I'm coming. You're my brother," he replied.

"I know you prefer to avoid these types of social engagements, though. So, really, it does mean a lot," his little brother insisted.

"Don't mention it. It's not everyday your brother graduates from medical school. I'm proud of you," he said.

...

"I'm so glad you're coming tonight," her friend said.

"Of course I'm coming. You're my best friend," she replied.

"I know, but you're always invited to all of these really exciting things by really important people and just knowing that you've chosen to come to my graduation ceremony instead of any of that really, really does mean a lot to me," her friend insisted.

"Don't mention it. We've been best friends since we were little kids. You're like a sister to me. I wouldn't miss it," she said.

...

He saw her sitting with a group of people. They looked well-dressed and important. She looked like a miracle. He felt something different within him. A longing so pure and alien that he smiled involuntarily at the newness.

She saw him approach her. He walked with an ease unfamiliar to her. His face wore comfort like a soft breath. He carried peace in his lips and a smile in his eyes. She felt something different within her. A calm so pure and alien that she gasped involuntarily at the newness.

"Will you honor me with a dance? " he asked.

"Yes, " she replied.

They danced in silence. He looked at the doubt in her eyes and beheld it like a mother beholds her frightened child. She looked at the compassion in his eyes and beheld it like the hand of a rescuer, offered to her in the rubble of a collapsed building.

"You smell like spring. You dance like water. You attract things within me I do not know how to explain. I want to spend many moments with you," he said.

"Yes... thank you... okay... " she replied.

They left the reception.

...

He sat alone and discontent. He couldn't read. the quiet felt like the weight of absence. He had never felt this way: uncomfortable within the cage of solitude. He was lonely. He missed her. He missed her in public. He missed her in private. When he awoke, he missed her. When he went to sleep, he missed her. He longed for nothing else and smiled at every thought of her.

She was surrounded by her friends and she was giddy. She was talking about him. The sounds of her voice were joy and satisfaction. She had never been this way. So full in ways she still didn't understand. There was nothing missing. She was full of him. His warmth comforted her heart and his words eased her mind. She awoke each morning looking forward to hearing his voice on the phone. She went to bed each night with his love keeping her dreams the sweetest company. She longed for nothing more and always smiled.

...

"I understand. "

www.ingramcontent.com/pod-product-compliance
Lightning Source LLC
Chambersburg PA
CBHW071248130626

46556CB00003B/1213